THE JOURNEY

DANI WILLIAMSON

The Journey

Copyright © 2025 by Dani Williamson.

MILTON & HUGO L.L.C.
4407 Park Ave., Suite 5
Union City, NJ 07087, USA

Website: *www. miltonandhugo.com*
Hotline: *1- 888-778-0033*
Email: *info@miltonandhugo.com*

Ordering Information:
Quantity sales. Special discounts are granted to corporations, associations, and other organizations. For more information on these discounts, please reach out to the publisher using the contact information provided above.

Library of Congress Control Number: 2025915113
ISBN-13:   979-8-89285-602-7   [Paperback Edition]
        979-8-89285-603-4   [Hardback Edition]
        979-8-89285-604-1   [Digital Edition]

Rev. date: 07/11/2025

ONE

Waiting and waiting and waiting. This hospital room sucks, this bed is uncomfortable, this paper gown is itchy, the walls are a drab beige color, and I'm so nervous I can feel my heart pounding in my chest. I look up to my husband, Levi, "I don't have a good feeling about the—" The doctor walks in shutting the door behind him. He turns to us with a look of remorse, "Mr. and Mrs. Kelsh, I don't have great news for you. Unfortunately you are unable to get pregnant." Levi left his standing position, sitting next to me on the bed, with a look of hurt he wrapped an arm around me. We have been trying for months to get pregnant, and every time we take the test, it is always negative. So we decided to come and see a doctor, to figure out why. "But why?" I asked and he looked at me sympathetically. "You have ripped vaginal tissue that did not heal properly, after what happened. Even though it was ten years ago, it has affected your ability to have children, and I am so sorry," he said. I look down at the scar I have on my arm from that night... *I looked up at the hooded stranger as he stood over me with the sharp silver weapon in hand. I swing my arm but he grabs it, taking the knife and running it deep down the length of my left arm...* I start to cry into Levi's chest. "You can change into your clothes now, try to have a good day. Once again I am sorry." he places a hand on mine and Levi's shoulders and then leaves the room. After

1

signing the release forms, we see the doctor as we walk towards the exit, "Thank you, Doctor Williams, we appreciate you." Levi shakes his hand. "Have a nice day you two. Goodbye." The doctor says and we go our separate ways.

"It's okay you know..." He pauses "...we could always adopt a child." Levi reassures. "Yeah, I know, but that still doesn't help how I feel about not being able to grow a beautiful child myself." Tears begin rolling down my cheeks. I turn my face and watch the passing trees as we near our house.

We arrived home as it began to rain. I watch the water drops roll down my window, what a great addition to this wonderful day of depression. Levi jumped out of the car to run and open the door. As he was jogging to the door, he tripped over the water hose that was laying on the ground, falling face-first into the soggy grass. A small smile formed on my face for a split second as seeing him fall was pretty funny. He quickly stands and unlocks the door. Walking back towards the car I can see that he has mud all over his face and the front of his shirt. I chuckle once more at the sight. "Are you okay, hon?" I question as he opens my door. "Never better." playfully rolling his eyes. "Maybe now you'll learn to put it away." Laughing, I slide out of the car and quickly walk inside, looking out for the water hose on my way. Levi walks into the house, mud prints trailing behind him onto the tile flooring. I give him a look and point to the mucky boots. He turns and takes them back outside. I walk up the stairs to change my soppy clothes. Standing naked in front of the mirror looking at my stomach, I start to imagine what it would be like to have a baby growing in there. Levi walks into the room and takes his clothes off, throwing them into the hamper, so he wouldn't be muddy any longer. Wrapping his arms around me he strokes my hair, I begin to cry again. "I know I shouldn't be crying so much about the situation but I can't help it." I wipe tears off my face. "Hey, look. You have every right to be upset about this. If you want to cry, then you have every right to, don't be sorry for feeling heartache." He twists me around, gives me a short kiss on my forehead, then goes to shower. I slide my closet door open and walk in. I take a pair of purple and blue cotton pajamas off the shelf and slide them onto my, now dry, body. I crawl into bed and try to get some sleep. I feel Levi slide into the covers about 20 minutes later, wrapping his arms around me and pulling my body towards him, he gives me a kiss on the back of my head and whispers "Goodnight, my love." I fell asleep.

I wake up the next morning to the smell of bacon and eggs. I turn my face away from the light that is peaking through the blinds and rub the sleep from my eyes. I glance at the digital alarm clock on the nightstand and read the time, 11:04 am. Tossing the warm covers off of my body, I stand and walk to the bathroom. As I remember the news we received yesterday I begin tearing up again, but push it back as I brush my teeth. "Ellie, you awake?" I see Levi pop his head through the door, in the mirror. "Yeah, in the bathroom." I rinse the toothpaste from my mouth and walk to him. "You made breakfast?" I hug him. "Yes, I did. Just for you." We walk down the steps and into the kitchen. I make a plate of food and take a seat at the table.

Once we both finished eating, Levi went upstairs and I start washing our dishes. As I finish drying the last dish, I hear a thud right above my head in the room that would have been the nursery for our baby. Curious, I silently make my way up to the room. The door is only slightly cracked open, just enough for me to hear the soft crying coming from my husband's lips. My heart shatters into a million little pieces for the second time in two days. Tears fill my eyes, and I knock and push the door open all the way. Levi looks up, saltwater streaming from his eyes. I see broken decor on the floor and a hole in the wall the size of a fist. I kneel in front of him and wipe the tears from his cheeks, just as he did mine yesterday. He pulls me into his lap. Holding each other for the next 20 minutes, mourning the child we can't bear. "I've been thinking about what you said yesterday," I start, "About adopting a child." Levi looks at me with shiny hopeful eyes, "I think it would be a good idea." I finish. "Really? That's great!" A slight smile forming on his lips as he tries to cheer up a bit. I love him so much.

A week later we find ourselves looking at adoption classes to take, and the next we are sitting in a room full of other people hoping to have what it takes to be a foster parent. About a month of biweekly classes we are finally ready to start with interviews. "Now, Mr. and Mrs. Kelsh, we have a few children that I feel like you would be interested in getting to know and possibly adopting, but let me get some of your information for background checks and we would need to examine your house and see if it is a suitable living situation for a child." Ms. Jones gathers some papers and hands us each a pen. "Oh, yes, ma'am we completely understand, that would not be a problem at all" I say taking the pin. After reading and signing the paper we hand it back and schedule a time for the caseworker to come and look at the house. "Your background checks should be back in the next 7-14 days. I will give you a call when they come in and from there we can set up a meeting with some of the children if everything looks good on the report." She informs us. "Do either of you have any questions about any of the paperwork or anything?" She questions as she puts our file to the side. "Actually I do have a question or two. When you say suitable for a child, are you talking about safety locks on cabinets and doors, or just to make sure we have everything we would need for a child?" I ask. "Well it would be both. You would need to have safety locks on anything dangerous or harmful to children. Make sure the kitchen knives are in a safe place where they cannot be reached by little fingers. You would need a room for the child to stay, and just to be safe get a small twin bed and a crib because you never know which you may need." She informs us. "We have a crib already and I also happen to have an extra bed that our niece uses when she stays over, so we have both of those covered. We will obviously wash the mattress and get new sheets and pillows. One more question i have is, do we need to have snacks and child food on hand? Or baby food or formula?" I ask feeling a little silly for my question. "No. You would get all of that once we have a placement for you, until then you should be fine." She says. We stand and say our thank yous and exit her office. The wood flooring creaks under our feet as we walk through the small building, passing through the front lobby and out of the wide double doors. We pass chatting people on the way to the car.

The entire ride home was completely silent, other than the low hum of the car engine and passing traffic. "Hey, Levi?" he turns into our driveway "Are you sure we are making the right decision...by adopting?" Putting the car in park and giving me a look of sympathy he replies "Yes, without a doubt. In my heart, I know that this is the right thing to do." Placing his right hand on my leg for comfort. "Try not to think too much about it right now. We have one to two weeks to think about this while waiting on our background checks to come through, and if by the time they do, and you've changed your mind..." he takes a deep breath, "...then we will wait." As a smile makes its way to my frowning face "You're right babe, you always know exactly what to say. Alright, I think we have been sitting in the driveway for long enough, let's go in." Walking up the staircase, I pause at the door that will be for our future child. I start to imagine all of the different themes this room will have as our child grows up and takes on new interests. My heart begins to warm at the idea of the sound little feet make against hardwood floors as they run and play. I finally continue past the door and into my bedroom to throw on some more comfortable clothes, before heading down to the kitchen to cook dinner. As I reach the bottom of the carpeted steps, I see Levi sitting at his desk working. He glances up at me, quickly smiles, blows me a kiss, and then returns to his work. I saunter off to the fridge and pull out the ingredients to make spaghetti.

TWO

It has been a long waiting game and took longer than 14 days for our background checks to come back. We have had multiple meetings with the adoption agency and children. These past couple of months have been super stressful. After getting our background checks back we started with the paperwork process, and with trying to figure out what all we needed to be considered for placement...like having child locks on all the cabinets, drawers, toilet seats, and even the ones that go on doorknobs... and many more requirements. We do not know the age of the child that we could be placed with so it is all just for extra safety. After coming home from the first meeting we had at the adoption agency, I have given a lot of thought to this whole adoption thing and I think it is the best thing for our lives, and not only our lives but a child's life as well. In preparing the house for a new addition, we had to turn Levi's office area into another bedroom so that we will be ready for a child of any age. Now we have a nursery with a crib and toys for any kid and a room for an older kid with a twin-sized bed, both with a solid neutral-colored bead spread since we are unsure of gender.

Standing in the doorway of what used to be the office space, I glance around looking at the perfectly made bed and the new curtains hanging in the window. I start getting nervous. What if this child doesn't like us? I push those feelings to the side and close the door to the room. As I walk down the stairs I hear a loud knock at the door. I met with Levi at the bottom of the steps. I cross my fingers and smile. Today is the final inspection before placement. All of the house prep and safety precautions we have been taking, are all for this day. The house has to be in perfect condition before we can get a placement. We open the door and greet the same lady from before. I cannot remember her name for the life of me.

"Good afternoon Mr. and Mrs. Kelsh. How are you two doing today?" She gives us a bright smile. "Good afternoon to you as well, Mrs. Wells. We are doing pretty good today, how about you?" My husband answers. He's always been good with names, unlike me. We go through the same interview questions as usual and then we take a tour of the house again like we have every other time. We are crossing our fingers in hopes that we pass this final inspection. Once we finish making our way through the house, we all sit around the table in the dining room. She folds her hand and looks down at her clipboard. "Well, I don't know how to tell you both this…" She takes a long pause, her face as serious as ever. My heart stops and I glance sideways at Levi. We didn't pass and now we will have to restart the whole process over again an- "But you have done a wonderful job with meeting all of the requirements and I am extremely happy to tell you that we can now begin the placement process." She interrupts my thoughts and gives us another big bright smile. "You had me thinking we failed! Are you trying to give us heart attacks?" I laugh and sigh in relief trying to slow my heart rate back down. "I do apologize Mrs. Kelsh, but that was funny you have to admit." She cracks another smile and we both agree with her. Once we have signed all of the necessary papers to move forward, we say our goodbyes. After the door shuts behind her I turn and face Levi. "We did it!" I cheer, and we both do a little happy dance, then he pulls me into his arms in a tight embrace. Now that we have the official green light we can finally stop stressing about household things. We still have about a week before we get our first placement and we will find out the age and gender on the day of arrival.

We spent the whole week grocery shopping and doing last-minute things around the house and in the yard. The night before we could hardly sleep, we were so excited to meet the child. We wake up early, eat breakfast and wait for our placement to show up. Finally a knock at the door, I jump up out of my seat and almost trip over my own feet trying to get to the door. "Slow down baby." Levi calms me. I gather myself and we walk over to the door and open it to find Mrs. Wells and a young girl hiding behind her.

"Hi, honey..." I bend down so I am eye-level with the small child, "My name is Ellie, but you can call me El." I hold out my hand to her. She slightly smiles and steps from behind Mrs. Wells. "My name is Melanie but I go by Mel, and this is Hopper." She holds up a stuffed turtle.

"Well, it is very nice to meet you both. This is my husband Levi." I look back at him then I lean in and whisper "But you can call him 'Stinky.'" She giggles. I stand back up "do you want to go check out the house and see your room?" I smile down at her. We all turn and walk in through the door. Her eyes go wide as she takes in everything. We get to the upstairs and I inform her she will have a room and a bed she does not have to share. "Yep, and I can paint it whatever color you want. We can go to the paint store later this week if you want to and you can choose whatever color you like." Levi adds, and her face lights up. "Even orange like the sunrise?" She questions "Most definitely, we can make it look like a sunrise if you want to." He smiles back at her. I can see on his face that he is happy

9

we decided to do this, and my heart swells. This is probably one of the best decisions we have made in our adult life. "Yes, I really like the sunrise." She hugs hopper close.

Once we finish the walk-through Mrs. Wells tells us a few last-minute reminders about the process and how it all works and informs us what date the check-in will be on. We say our goodbyes once she makes sure Melanie is settled in, then she leaves.

THREE

A few weeks go by and everything is going well with Mel. Yes, we have had some ups and downs, but for the most part, everything is great. It is nearing the time for our check-in visit so we are cleaning up the house. I hear the doorbell ring, Levi is in his office so I walk over to answer it, leaving Mel sitting in her bright pink bean bag chair watching cartoons. I open it to find a woman I have never seen before. She is wearing a black collared polo shirt and khaki pants, holding a clipboard, seeming regular but also out of place. There is something familiar about her but I am sure we have never crossed paths.

"Hello, can I help you?" I say, not fully opening the door.

"Uh yes ma'am, I am here for the check-in." She looks past me and into the house.

"Please excuse me, but I thought Mrs. Wells would be doing the check-in?" I question. Her eyes bolt to mine.

"She is sick, and will be out of the office for a while, so I am temporarily filling in for her."

"Oh, well okay. Please, come in." I step aside, opening the door enough for her to enter. "What is your name?" I close the door.

"Laura. Where is Melody?" She answers, then questions while her eyes bolt around looking for Mel.

"You mean Melanie? She is in the den watching cartoons." I inform her with confusion on my face and lead the way.

"Yes, right Melanie. They sound so similar I get them confused." She says following close behind. We make it to the den, Mel no longer in her bean bag chair but now laying on the couch. She must be getting sleepy.

"Hey, Mel." I walk over to her. She looks up at me and then directly behind me.

"Miss Laura?" She jumps up. "I thought you went away?" She questions and hugs her.

"Hey, Melody. I moved for a little while but I missed this place so much I had to come back." She hugs her back. Okay so Mel knows this lady, but she keeps calling her 'Melody', I am more than confused.

"It's Melanie! You always do that." She laughs up at the woman.

Looking up from the child and facing me again, "Could you give us a few minutes? I need to question her without you or your husband present." I didn't even realize he had joined us. I grab his hand then we both turn and leave the den, but neither of us wanders too far.

"Who is that? Where is Wells?" Levi asks in a hushed voice.

"Apparently she is sick, and Laura," I point behind me "is filling in for her until she gets better. But it is weird because she keeps calling Melanie 'Melody'."

"That is strange"

"Mel obviously knows her, and she said that she always calls her by the wrong name. I just don't get it." I shrug. We both strain to hear what they are talking about but can't hear anything. We sit at the dining room table and wait for about 30 minutes before Miss Laura comes in to speak with us.

"Alrighty. Melody seems to be happy, but I have a few concerns." She takes a seat across from us. I glance at Levi and he at me.

"Is she getting fed regularly and the proper amount?" Furrowing her brows she looks back and forth between us.

"Yes absolutely. She eats three meals a day and they have the proper food groups and we make sure not to even buy the foods she is allergic to, so there is no chance she can get to it." Levi informs firmly but not in a rude way.

"Please do not take offense to the question, sir. I-" Levi cuts her off.

"She also gets two small snacks a day. One between breakfast and lunch and another between lunch and dinner. So I would like to know why you even ask that question, Miss Laura." I place my hand on his shaking leg under the table to calm him down a little.

"I do apologize, but I only ask because she is very skinny looking."

"If I may," I start "She is 10, correct? Kids her age have a high metabolism, plus she is constantly outside running and playing. So it is normal for her at this age to look like she does. When I was her age I was about the same size as she is and I did not gain weight until I was nearly 13. She is no smaller than she was the day she arrived, so I believe she is healthy, but if it would put your mind at ease about her size, we can make a doctor's appointment to get her a checkup." I finish and I feel Levi's leg still.

"I understand what you are saying, but yes it would put my mind at ease for her to get a checkup done. Once you schedule the appointment contact me here," she hands me a business card with her information on it, "and let me know the time and place so I can put it in her file." She stands.

"Is that it?" I question.

"For this visit, yes. You both have a wonderful rest of your day. I can show myself out, thank you." She walks out the front, closing the door behind her.

"Well, I thought this check-in would go differently. That was a little strange, wasn't it?" Levi's leg begins to shake again.

"Yes, very." We both join Mel back in the den. I put the TV on mute.

"Hey, Mel. How do you know Miss Laura?" I sit on the coffee table across from where she is sitting on the couch, Levi on the chair off to the left of me.

"She would help the ladies at the place we stayed in. She would make our beds and she would take us to the supper table and she also would make sure we brush our teeth before bed. She would tell me that I am her favorite but she always always called me Melody and not Melanie." She explains.

"And when you said she went away, was there a reason? Do you know?" I question.

"Well I know one time she got into trouble because she wanted to take me out for ice cream and not the other girls. They said she was not allowed to take any of us off the property without the congrimation from Mrs. Jones." She informs us.

"You mean confirmation from Mrs. Jones?" I let out a small laugh at the adorable way she mispronounced the word.

"Yes. After that, I didn't see her again and all the grownups told me she had to go away. But now she is back." She smiles brightly.

"Okay, we were just wondering. You can continue to watch TV." She lays back down looking sleepy once again.

"Do you want a blanket?" Levi stands holding the blanket that was placed on the back of the chair he was in.

"Yes, please."

He places the blanket over her and I turn the volume on the TV back on. We walk out of the den, Levi heading back to his office while I head to the kitchen to make Mel a second snack and start prepping for dinner. I walk into the den to see if she was still awake, but she was not so I placed her snack in the refrigerator. She can have it when she wakes up or save it for tomorrow. Once I have the steaks we are eating for dinner marinating, I start washing and roughly peeling potatoes, cut them into chunks then soak them in salt water for about an hour. After I have most of the food prepared I go and check on Mel again, still sleeping. I walk up the stairs and knock on the door of Levi's office, then enter.

"Hey, baby." He looks up from his computer.

"Hey," I say, closing the door behind me. "We should go ahead and make that doctor's appointment for Mel. Do you remember if Mrs. Wells or Mrs. Jones said anything about having a preferred pediatrician for the children?" I sit in a chair across from his desk.

"Uhm not that I can recall, no."

"Okay. Do you want to take her or do you want me to or both of us?"

"I would love to but you might have to do it alone because I have a lot of work to do this week. But I want to know everything about it."

"Okay, that is fine. I definitely will tell you everything, though I'm pretty positive she is not malnourished." I roll my eyes with the last word as it leaves my mouth.

"Me too. There was absolutely no reason for Laura to question that. To me, Mel doesn't look underweight for her age at all." Also rolling his eyes at the situation. "I have a feeling that there is more to the story about why she "'went away'", and she was kind of sketchy when she was here. She only questioned Mel and she didn't complete another walkthrough. Which I thought was going to happen to make sure we are accommodating her properly. She also didn't ask us any questions about how the past few weeks have been or anything of the sort."

"My thoughts exactly. I just don't understand. I've got to call Mrs. Jones to see if they have a preferred pediatrician, and how I need to go about making an appointment since she is legally not ours yet and we don't have insurance on her, so I'll ask if the check-in is split into a couple of days or what."

"Sounds like a good plan to me." He replies. I stand and kiss him before exiting, closing the door behind me. I look down at the time and I believe it is too late to call Mrs. Jones's office right now, so I will have to do so in the morning. I walk back downstairs and hear Mel talking to someone. Once I hit the last step I see her standing at the door.

"Mel, who's at the door?" I walk over and open it a little more. I see Laura standing there. My brows furrow.

"How can I help you? Did you leave something here?" I pat Mel on top of her head and she walks behind me.

"Oh uh. No, I just wanted to talk to Melody again."

"You mean Melanie." I state.

"Yes, right, Melanie."

"Okay, well your questions can wait until the next check-in. We are about to start making dinner, and it's a little late in the evening for a pop-up visit. Have a good day." I close the door, turning to Mel.

"What was she asking you?" Crouching down to be at eye level with her.

"She was trying to get me to go get candy with her because I am still her favorite. But I told her that I can't leave without talking to you or Stinky first."

16

"That was a smart thing to say. Next time will you come to get me or Levi if someone is at the door, please?"

"Yes ma'am."

"Thank you. Now dinner won't be ready for a while, do you want to eat your snack now or do you want to save it for tomorrow?" I stand back up.

"Can I just eat some of it now, and the rest tomorrow?"

"You sure can my darling. Come sit at the table and I'll grab it for you." She sat and ate part of her snack while I started cooking. Levi came down after finishing a few more emails and got the grill going. We ate Steak and mashed potatoes with green beans, then watched a movie.

FOUR

LEVI

I woke up on the couch, the TV no longer playing. I squint my eyes to see the digital clock on the microwave in the kitchen, 3:22 am. Rubbing my eyes I slowly sit up and stretch, then glance at Ellie and Melanie. They both look so peaceful. My heart fills with love, as I look at my wife and then at Mel. I've gotten to know this little girl and everything about her over the past several weeks and I just can't wait to be able to officially adopt her. Leaving Ellie on the couch, I pick Mel up and carry her to her room tuck her into bed then shut the door. I get to the couch and carry El up to our room next. I go back downstairs to grab a glass of water. As I'm filling a glass with water, I glance out the kitchen window into the backyard and in the moonlight, I see an outline of a person, head tilted up at one of the top-floor rooms. Dropping the glass into the sink, I rush to the back door on the other side of the den. As I fling the door open I stand there confused. I no longer see the figure. Searching the yard from where I'm standing, I see nothing out of the ordinary. Maybe I saw a shadow of something, It is dark and I am still half asleep. I shut the door, locking it again. I must be going crazy, but just in case, I walk the whole house making sure all of the doors and windows are locked and secure. Heading back to my room I decide it's best if I don't mention any of that to El.

FIVE

ELLIE

I wake up in my bed the next morning. Levi must have carried me up here. Which means he also carried Mel to her room, and that is the cutest thing ever. He was so meant to be a dad. How he is with Mel, makes me love him more if that is even possible. I roll over and see Levi sleeping still. I quietly get up and walk downstairs, and begin to make breakfast. I pull out eggs, bacon, and bread to make breakfast sandwiches. I glance out of the window to see the sun slowly rising more and more. Mel's favorite colors fill the sky and then slowly fade as I continue cooking.

"It smells super yummy in here." I hear a little voice behind me.

"Super yummy." Repeated a deeper voice. I turn to see Levi pick Mel up and give her good morning kisses and hugs.

"Well thank you my loves!" I kiss them both, then grab some grapes and blueberries out of the refrigerator.

Once I have the fruit washed and the rest of the food cooked, we begin to make our breakfast sandwiches. Mel pours syrup on top of her eggs and bacon and then smashes it flat between two slices of toast. Levi does the same but with ketchup.

"EWW!" Mel's face twists into one of disgust "Stinky, that is nasty!" she laughs.

"You don't know that if you don't try it, silly girl." He holds it up for her to take a bite and she turns her face away "No way."

"You know what is good on it? Mayonnaise." I say as I spread it onto both slices of toast I have.

"I want to try!" She leans over and takes a bite of mine.

"You'll try the one with mayo on it, but not ketchup?" Levi hangs his mouth open in fake disbelief.

"Yep." She chirps back, giggling.

Once we finish breakfast Levi takes Mel upstairs to get washed up and out of her pajamas. I wash the dishes, then grab my phone and head outside to call Mrs.Jones. She answers after a few rings.

"Hey, it's Ellie Kelsh." I inform her.

"Good morning Ellie. How is everything going?" She asks cheerfully.

"It's going good, I just have a few questions and concerns." I begin to pace back and forth.

"Okay, let's hear it." Sounding attentive.

"Is there a certain doctor that Mel needs to go see for a checkup? And how would I go about setting up an appointment since she isn't legally our child yet?"

"You would have to call me and get it set up, we just recently changed that. But Mel just had her annual checkup and is perfectly healthy for her age. May I ask why you want to have her seen?"

"Well, yesterday we had our check-in visit. Levi and I were asked if we had been feeding her properly. She said it was because Mel looks too skinny, but to me, she looks normal for her age." I explain.

"In my notes here Melanie's most recent visit to the doctor was the day before she came to you two. That question makes no sense. It should have been in the notes on her file."

"Well, that was also the only question Miss Laura had asked an-"

"I'm sorry. Who?"

"Miss Laura." I state, "She said that Mrs. Wells is out sick and that she is filling in for her. We were a bit confused about it, but Mel seems to know her and says she used to work there. Which is weird because she keeps calling her-"

"Melody." She finishes for me.

"So she does work there?"

"You haven't heard from Mrs. Wells at all?"

"No ma'am. Does Laura still work there?"

"No. She used to. She always favored Melanie over the other children, and she has called her Melody since the day we got her into our care. Some things happened and Laura was fired, and never allowed to return."

"What happened?" That came out a little harsher than I had meant.

"She had a daughter that passed away when she was Melanie's age. She is the spitting image of her too, but impossible that there is any relation. Laura thinks that Melanie is her daughter that has come back to life. She tried to take her from the home. Her daughter's name was-"

"Melody." It was I that had cut her off this time. "So how is she back? How did she even know we have her?"

"I have no idea. She has been in a mental hospital for the past 8 months because she went crazy over not being able to see Melanie. She tried to break in several times to take her. And she was talking to people that weren't there. She must have gotten out somehow. As for her knowing where you live and that you have Melanie, I honestly have no idea. She was good friends with Jen, Mrs. Wells, and must have gone to her when she got out. And knowing Jen, she probably let her stay there."

"So someone needs to check on Mrs. Wells if this lady is crazy and trying to take Mel. She showed up a few hours after leaving and was trying to get Mel to leave with her. The police should go over to Mrs. Wells's house to check on her."

"I will get this handled, you should not be involved." I hear papers rustling on her end.

"Shouldn't get involved?" I say loudly "This lady has been in my house! I most definitely am already involved, especially since this is my family." I state. Levi places a hand on my shoulder. I jump a little.

"I saw someone out here last night." He says looking around the yard.

"Hold on Mrs. Jones. What did you say?" I ask him to repeat himself even though I heard what he said.

"After I carried you and Mel up to bed, I came down to get some water. I saw a figure out here and it looked like they were facing upwards towards the second-floor windows. I dropped my cup and came out here as quickly as possible but saw nothing when I opened the door."

"Why did you not tell me?"

"It was 3 am, dark and I was sleepy. I thought I was just seeing things. But now that I've heard some of your conversation, I probably wasn't just seeing stuff." He gives me a look of worry.

"Did you hear that Mrs. Jones?" I turn back to the phone.

"Yes, I did. You need to get Melanie away from the house. Tell her that you all are going on a fun little trip. I will call the police." She hangs up before I can say anything else.

I look at Levi, "I guess we are going on a trip." We calm ourselves down and walk back inside to Mel.

"Mel! Melanie!" I call as I walk up the stairs.

"Yes?" She pops around the corner as I reach the top.

"Do you want to go on a fun trip?" I take her hand and walk her into her room.

"Yes, yes, yes a million billion times yes!" She says excitedly.

"Great! Let's pack a bag, shall we?" I bend down and reach underneath her bed, grab her suitcase, and pull it out. She grabs her favorite pair of pajamas and throws them in first, then clean underwear, and socks.

"Okay Mel, we need some regular clothes too." I stand and grab some outfits from her closet, fold them and place them in the bag as well. I find a few pairs of her shoes and set them right on top, then zip it.

"Well, that was the fastest bag packing I've ever seen!" I give her a high-five. "I'm going to pack my bag now hun. Do you want to help me?" I do not want her out of my sight right now. We make it to the master bedroom and Levi is packing his bag.

"Hey, my girls. I was thinking we could drive down to Akron. We can go to the art museum, the zoo, and the parks, how does that sound?" He questions us.

"That sounds awesome!" Mel jumps up and down clapping with excitement.

"That sounds like a great plan to me." I grab my suitcase from inside my closet and begin packing. Once I get my clothes from the closet, I carry the suitcase into the room and grab my pajamas from my dresser. "Don't forget to grab Hopper, Mel." I state as i zip my bag. Once we finish packing, we load everything into the car and start our hour drive from Warren to Akron.

SIX

I look up hotels around the area of Akron during our drive and make a reservation online for about three days.

"I've got a hotel booked for three nights. We can check in when we get there, set our things down, then we can go eat." I grab Levi's hand and squeeze. I turn my head and see Mel looking at all of the passing buildings.

"Can we eat somewhere where they have cheeseburgers?" She turns to look at me.

"We sure can." I answer. She goes back to looking out of her window.

It was a silent car ride, for the most part. Levi glanced at Mel, in the rearview mirror every so often. I look out of my window. I feel Levi grab my hand so I turn my head, he gestures back to Mel. I turn my head to see her sleeping. Head hanging forward and her body slumped. I reach my hand back and tilt her head back up and lean her against the window so she won't have pain in her neck later. I face back forward once I finish adjusting her head, and take Levi's hand again.

"What do you think is going to happen?" my eyes straight.

"I honestly don't know. We can only hope for the best. Have you heard anything from Mrs. Jones since this morning?"

"No, not really. She gave me her personal phone number, so I will ask." I pull out my phone and dial her number.

"Hello." She answers after a couple of rings.

"Hey, it's Ellie. I was calling to see if there is any update on anything. And what did the police say?"

"I told them the situation directly affects one of the children we have that is currently in your care. They said they are going to send a patrol car out to your house and someone will drive by every hour. I told them that you were going out of town for a few days with Melanie. It is best she remain in your care since Laura knows every way in and out of the children's home."

"Okay. When we get back do we need to go to the police station and speak to someone?"

"Yes, I was just getting ready to tell you that. They also have yours and Levi's information, and should be reaching out to you either later today or tomorrow." She informs me.

"Alright. Please keep me updated if anything happens. Did they send someone to Mrs. Wells house?"

"Yes. They did not see Jen. No one was home. I still can't get a hold of her on her cell though."

"I don't think we should come back until we know that Laura isn't going to bother us anymore. I can work from home, and so can Levi. Mel isn't in school because it is summer, so I think we'll just travel for a week or so."

"I understand that. We can do check-in over video call just so we can keep up with the adoption."

"That sounds good to me. Please keep me updated, bye"

"Will do, goodbye." She hangs up.

I turn to Levi, "did you hear that?" he nods his head in agreement.

"I think after our three days in Akron, we should drive further, maybe to Columbus? They have a lot to do there too." I say showing him pictures on my phone.

"That sounds like a good idea to me. I don't care where we go as long as my family is safe." He grabs my hand, raising it to his lips and giving me a little kiss.

"I agree. We will be good." I bring his hand to my mouth and kiss his hand. "How much further do we have? I need to pee." letting go of his hand trying to see the GPS.

"Uhh, I think we have about 30 more minutes. I can pull over at a gas station, Mel probably needs to go too." He pulls into the nearest gas station. I get out and walk to the other side of the car where Mel is sleeping. I open the door slowly.

"Hey Mel, wake up baby." I gently move her body to help wake her.

"Are we there yet?" Voice quiet.

"No, we are at a gas station. Let's go use the restroom." I unbuckle her and help her out of the vehicle. She squints her eyes at the outside sun and covers her eyes. We all three walk in and I take Mel to the restrooms, and Levi gets some drinks and snacks.

We finish our business and then wash our hands. As we are leaving the restroom Mel looks up at me, with questioning eyes.

"Do you have a question?" I ask and stop walking. I bend down so I can be at eye level with her. She opens her mouth like she wanted to ask me a question but then shakes her head no. "You can ask me or tell me anything."

"We aren't on vacation are we?"

"What do you mean? Of course, we are."

"The last time I saw Miss Laura, I had to stay inside away from her. Now I seen her again and we are leaving."

"Oh honey, it's okay. There are a few things that Miss Laura is not allowed to do and she is trying to do them. We are going away on a little vacation so that Miss Laura can do what she is supposed to do and not get into trouble." I can't tell her this lady is crazy.

"Okay." I stand back up and we walk over to where Levi is, and he picks Mel up. He finishes checking out and we head back to the vehicle. We finally get back on the road and just listen to music.

We finally make it to our hotel and check-in. We take all of our things to the room and settle in for a moment before heading out to eat. I change Melanie's clothes since she had spilled some of her drink on herself during the ride up here. I threw my hair in a messy bun and we head out of the door. We pulled into the parking lot of the restaurant, and we walk in.

"How many in your party?" The hostess greets us.

"Two adults and a child." Levi answers. We follow her to our table, she informs us that our waiter will be with us shortly, we thank her and she leaves us. As we are looking over the menu our waiter walks up.

"Good evening, my name is Dann, I'll be serving you all today. What would we like to drink?"

"Water."

"Coke, please."

"And what would you like cutie." He turns to Mel.

"Can I have a Sprite, please?"

"You absolutely can. Would we like to order any appetizers?"

"Cheese sticks!" Mels says quickly.

"We will have the cheese sticks then." I lightly laugh.

"Alrighty, I will go put in your drinks and apps, then I'll be right back."

"Awesome, thank you." I reply then he walks away.

"Do you know what you want to eat, Mel?" Levi asks.

"Cheeseburger with french fries." She smiles up at him. "Do you want to play tic-tac-toe with me?" She questions him.

"I absolutely do, but you, my dear, are going to lose." He picks up one of the crayons she is not using and they begin to play. I look over the menu to figure out what I want to eat, while they play. Our waiter comes back with our drinks and takes the rest of our order. Once we get all of our food we just eat and talk about random things.

Back in the car, we are all tired and ready for some rest. It has been a long day. I drive us back to the hotel so Levi can sit in the back with Mel, per her request. Waiting at a stop light, I just slowly look around at all of the gas stations and stores. My eyes see something as I turn my head, that made me do a double-take. I swear I saw Laura standing on the side of the road, but when I looked again I saw nothing. The light turns green and I drive on. This lady is in my head, that's the only explanation. There is no way she knows we left, let alone where we are. I tell myself to calm down and try to control my breathing. We make it back to the hotel and our room. We all change into our pajamas and crawl into bed.

SEVEN

I quickly jerk awake from the terrible dream I was just having. I look over and see Mel stir a little from the movement of the bed but she does not wake up. Levi, however, does wake up. He sits up with me and just wraps his arms around my body.

"It's okay. We are safe." It's like he knows what my dream was about. He hasn't said anything to me about it, but I know he thinks about it all of the time just like I do.

"I dreamt that she was here. While I was driving us back earlier I swear I thought I saw her, but when I looked again I didn't." He just holds me tighter and kisses the back of my head. He lays back, bringing me with him. I twist so that I am facing him, though I cannot see him I can feel him looking at me. He leans down and kisses my forehead.

The next day comes slowly for me. I feel like I did not get any sleep at all, but today I am determined to get my mind off of this whole Laura thing, even if it is just for a little while. I want to have fun with Mel, and my husband, and just be a happy little family with no worries. So today we are going to the art museum and the zoo. We get up around 9 am and get ready to head out. While I was putting on my clothes I get a call from a number I do not recognize so I ignore it. Once it stops ringing another call from the same number comes through. I roll my eyes and answer it.

"Hello?" I get nothing in response, so I hang up and block calls from that number. With all of the weird things happening right now, I do not need any more stress added to it.

Once we are ready, we make sure we have the room keys and everything we need then leave. We stop for breakfast first and then make our way to the museum and then the zoo.

Ending our day of fun we stop and grab something for dinner and head back to the room to relax and eat. I keep getting a strange feeling in my gut but I am unsure why. I push it down and do my best to ignore it. There is no reason for me to feel like this when we are safe. Once we finish eating we all lay in the bed cuddled up and watching movies until we all fall asleep.

EIGHT

LEVI

Hearing a big banging sound outside of our room, I jolt awake. Ellie and Mel wake as well. Mel wraps her arms around me and hides her face in my shirt. I wrap my arms around her and Ellie and give them a quick squeeze. I press my finger to my lips, "sshh," and slowly stand up out of the bed. Leaving Mel to wrap her arms around my wife, using her as safe arms to be in. I walk over to the door and look through the peephole. I don't see anything in the hallway, so I slowly open the door but not too much. I poke my head through and examine the hall. Looking left, then right. A few doors down I see a man with a cart, looking down at some things that were on the ground. Figuring he had just dropped a few of the things he was now picking up, I close our door and lock it back. I turn around and in the dim light, coming from the cracked bathroom door, I can see Ellie and Mel waiting for me to give them some reassurance.

"Everything is good. It looks like one of the workers had dropped a few things out in the hallway just a few doors down." I crawl back into the bed, wrapping my left arm around both of my girls. Once I get settled back into bed I hear a knock at the door. I groan quietly to myself and stand back up. Who is knocking this late at night anyway? I look through the peephole once again. This time I see someone. The worker that had made the loud noise. I slowly open the door but not all the way.

"Can I help you?" I ask quietly to not disturb anyone around us. He doesn't say anything. He just hands me a slip of paper and walks back down the hall to his cart. Puzzled, I unfold the small paper and read 'YOU cannot HIDE from ME.- L.S'. I close the door and make sure to lock it. What in the hell is this supposed to mean? I do not have a good feeling about it though. I see Ellie sitting up in the bed with a questioning look on her face. I walk over and hand her the note.

NINE

ELLIE

Taking the folded slip of paper from Levi, I read over it and am now more confused than I was before. "Is this a threat? I don't know what Lauras' last name is but I have a sick feeling this is her." How would she have found us? And knows what hotel and even our room number. This is getting out of hand. The police have no clue where she is.

"We will call tomorrow. Right now we need rest." Levi climbs back into the bed for the third time. Soon I can hear his faint snores, but I can't make my body sleep. Eventually, sleep does overcome me. Morning comes soon. I wake up still tired but we have things to handle today. I look over in bed and see that Levi and Mel are both gone. My initial thought was that something bad happened to him and then a more rational thought crossed my mind. They are probably down in the lobby and will be back soon. As I finish my thought the door opens with a smiling Mel and Levi with a hand full of brown paper bags. Mel does not hold the door open for Levi and it closes back on him, almost dropping the bags.

"Oops, I'm sorry!" Mel quickly apologizes and grabs a bag out of his hand. Once they are both in the room the door gets closed and locked. I quickly realize that the bags contained breakfast and there is also coffee in a cup holder. We sit around the little desk thing in the room and eat. I will talk to Mrs. Jones after we finish and clean up. As I sip my latte I begin to think about what is going to happen when the police get Laura and we go home. What if they don't allow us to adopt Mel? We were supposed to be placed with other children at some point, but I've already grown so attached to her. Judging by the way my husband is currently tearing apart his pancakes a making different animal shapes with them for Mels' entertainment, I can tell he has gotten attached to her too.

As I am lost in thought my ringing phone brings me back to an unfortunate reality. I look at the caller ID, Mrs. Jones. I quickly answer it.

"Mrs.Jones, hello."

"Hey, Ellie. How are things today? How is Melanie doing with the situation?"

"Good. Still unaware about everything happening and I plan to keep it that way for as long as I can."

"Good, good. So a detective just called and informed me that it looks like Laura hasn't been at Jen's house in a while, actually, no one has. Not even Jen. The police still have not seen her and I still cannot get ahold of her. I am getting really worried." She informs me.

"What is Laura's last name?"

"Her last name is Pierson, and has been for the last 28 years. But I believe her maiden name is Samuels. She has used Pierson since she got married at 18. Why do you ask?"

"We received a note last night from a worker at the hotel we are at and it was signed L.S. and I had a feeling it was her." After getting off the phone, I give Levi a look confirming that Laura's last name does start with S. I get up and start packing all of our things up. We are supposed to be checking out tomorrow but I plan on getting out of here now. If she already knows where we are and what room we are in, then we are not safe. Once I gather all of our things I put our bags beside the door and finish off my latte and my muffin. We walk down and load all of our belongings into the trunk of the car. Mel and I stay seated with the doors locked as Levi goes in to inform the front desk we are checking out early and get a refund for the last day.

We begin our drive back home, seeing as she already knows where we are and is following us, there is no reason for us to journey farther from Warren. If something were to happen to any of us that far from home, there's no telling what would happen. The best thing for Mel is for us to be back home where the police already know the situation and can have us protected at all times.

Once we finally make it back home, there is already an officer waiting for us at the front. We allow him to walk in first just to make sure everything is safe. Once we are cleared to go in, he informs us that the police department will have officers on rotating shifts so that there is always someone here to protect us. And if we leave they will follow us wherever we go.

"Thank you so much for taking the time to help us." I tell the officer. "Anything to protect the children." He flashes me a smile and walks back to his patrol car. He stays for about another hour in front of our house. Then another officer comes to relieve him. We will go to the police station tomorrow and turn in the note that we got in Akron and talk about what our next steps should be.

"Alright Mel, it's time to brush your teeth and get ready for bed." I state as I'm walking into the den. She rubs her sleepy eyes and nods "okay" as she slowly walks up the steps. We are all worn out from all the driving, hopefully we can finally get some sleep. Once we are all in bed it does not take long for sleep to come. We awake the next morning to the doorbell ringing. I walk down stairs and answer the door. It's the mailman. "Hello?" I question because he always just drops it in the box.

"Hey Mrs. Kelsh, I have this letter for you." He hands me an envelope with my name on it, then turns and leaves. Wondering why he handed it to me directly I shut the door. I open it and find a letter. "The police will not get me. I am always watching. I can always find Melody-L.S" "Levi!" I call up to him as I walk up the steps. I meet him in the hall and hand him the note. His face fills with confusion as he reads it. "She knows our mailman. He is the one that gave it to me at the door." I look at him. "We need to go to the police station now." He states. We go back up to our room and get dressed and call Mrs. Jones. She will come sit with Mel until we get back from the police station.

Once we get there we talk to a detective and give him both of the letters we have received from Laura. And they just tell us what we already know, stay inside, keep an eye on Mel, and don't talk to Laura if she shows up. We head back to the house and there are now two police cars out front, I glance over at Levi and we both hop out as soon as the car is in park.

"Is there a problem?" Levi asks as we open the front door. Two officers turn to look at us "oh, no sir. Wen just came in to chat with Mrs. Jones about the case." I nod and then go into the kitchen. I start making lunch for us. The officers say their goodbyes, then go sit back out in their cars out front. I finish up lunch and we all eat. Mrs.Jones stays for a while and we all chat about everything that's happening with Mel.

"I know this is not what you both had in mind when you first decided to adopt, and I am truly sorry that it has been this way. I see the way you both are caring for Mel and how she has become attached to you through these past couple of months. I believe once we get this Laura situation sorted out and behind us…" she pauses, "…I want to place Mel with you permanently." She smiles.

Levi and I look at each other and I make a sigh of relief. "That would be amazing." I beam and Levi is quick to agree. "We just don't know how long this situation is going to last, which sucks." I slouch back into the couch. "I know but from what the officers were telling me they have an idea of where she might be. They have been combing through traffic cameras and public bus cameras to find her and they have, so now they are tracking her movements that way. Still no sight of Jen, but they are hoping to find her wherever Laura has been hiding." She informs us. That's a lot of information to take in all at once. I place my fingers on my temples and rub my head. "Okay. So hopefully all of this will end soon. That's what I'm going to focus on." I place my hands back into my lap. "And getting Mel." Levi adds to what I said. I point my finger at him in agreement, "yes and getting Mel."

Mrs.Jones stays for about another hour then she leaves. By this point it's now dinner time and I think we all need to eat and get some well-deserved sleep. I get up to make dinner and as I'm cooking I get a phone call. I put down the tongs and ask Levi to watch the chicken. I step outside and answer.

"Hello?"

"This is detective Robert's with the warren police department, I'm looking for Ellie?"

"This is her. Has something happened?" I ask worriedly

"Yes ma'am. We have found Laura and have her in custody."

"Thank God. What about Mrs. Wells, Jen?"

"We also found her and she is currently being transported to the hospital. She is breathing but was not conscious when we found her. You will have to go to the hospital for more information. But I wanted to personally deliver the good news. Your family is now safe."

"What is going to happen with Laura?" I quickly question before he hangs up.

"Well she will be going to a maximum security mental facility, and she will get the treatment she needs. And if she improves she will then be sent to trial and imprisoned. All of that is not set in stone but that is the plan as of now. And the rest depends on how she responds to treatment, she may never get out of the maximum security facility."

"Thank you very much. Have a good night." I hang up and run back inside. I tell Levi the good news while crying tears of joy. He pulls me into a tight hug and kisses the top of my head. "We can finally be a family." He says into my hair and I nod against his chest and squeeze tighter. I finish cooking and we eat. Then we stay up and watch a family movie, one that Mel picked out of course.

TEN

Today is the day we have our final court hearing about the adoption for Mel. We are all so excited. The judge goes through his statement and when he finally gets to the end he stands. "Melanie you are now officially adopted by Levi and Ellie Walsh. You make such a beautiful family and I wish you all the best of luck." He sits back down but Levi and I jump up and smush Mel in a big hug. We finally have our own little family, and though it was hard, this amount of love and happiness is definitely worth the journey.

EPILOGUE

MELANIE'S BACKSTORY

TROUBLED PAST

Melanie had already lived in four different homes before she turned ten.

Her mother had disappeared when Melanie was just a toddler — no one ever gave her a clear answer why. Her father tried for a while, but things were always hard: missed bills, strange people in and out of the apartment, too many nights when dinner was a bag of chips and a can of soda. One day, he just didn't come home.

Melanie was found sitting alone on the floor of their apartment, her stuffed turtle wrapped in a towel like a baby. She didn't cry when the social worker came. She just asked if the turtle could come too.

She was moved into foster care — a string of temporary homes where she learned how to be quiet, helpful, invisible. If she was too loud, she got sent away. If she got too sad, they called someone else to deal with it.

At her third home, one of the foster parents kept the bedroom door locked from the outside. Melanie still doesn't talk about what happened there — just that Hopper, her turtle, "protected her" and "told her to stay quiet."

By the time she arrived at the orphanage, she didn't trust anyone. She didn't smile much. She didn't speak unless she had to. But she watched everything. Especially the adults.

That's when Miss Laura took an interest in her — too much interest. She called Melanie by the wrong name: Melody. At first, it seemed like a mistake. But then Laura started saying things like, "You're mine," and "You remind me of someone I lost." She offered gifts, attention, promises.

When Laura tried to take her out of the building without permission, Melanie said no.

It was one of the few times she used her voice.

After that, things started unraveling.

Melanie was transferred again — this time into emergency care. She had nothing but a duffel bag, Hopper, and the quiet ache of hoping someone, somewhere, would choose her... and mean it.

ONE

THE NEW PEOPLE

I was hiding a little behind Miss Jen. My hands were squeezing Hopper, my turtle. He's green and soft and never leaves me, not even when I sleep.

We were standing at this big door, and I didn't know what to expect. I had been to new houses before. Some nice, some not-so-nice. But this one felt... different. Quiet. Not scary, just... big.

A lady opened the door. She had warm eyes and a soft voice. She bent down and smiled at me.

"Hi, honey. My name is Ellie, but you can call me El," she said.

I peeked out from behind Miss Jen. "My name is Melanie but I go by Mel... and this is Hopper," I said shyly, holding him up.

"It's very nice to meet you both," she said, then turned to a tall man behind her. "This is my husband, Levi." She leaned toward me and whispered, "But you can call him 'Stinky.'"

I laughed, just a little. Not loud. Just a tiny giggle. "Hi, Stinky."

Levi made a funny face like he was pretending to be mad, but not really. I could tell he was trying to make me laugh more.

Ellie smiled again and asked, "Do you want to see your room?"

I nodded. My heart was thumping, but not in a bad way.

Inside, everything was clean and smelled like candles. The kind that smell like cookies. I followed them up the stairs and saw a bed. A whole bed just for me. No other kids. No sharing. Ellie said I could paint the room however I wanted.

"Even orange like the sunrise?" I asked.

"Most definitely," Levi said. "We can make it look like a sunrise if you want to."

And I believed him.

TWO

THE FIRST NIGHT

After Miss Jen left, it was just me, Ellie, and Stinky. I was nervous, but they didn't act scary or weird. Ellie helped me unpack my clothes and asked if I wanted to wear my pajamas already.

"They're soft and have little bunnies on them," I told her. She said that sounded perfect.

We ate dinner at a real table. Ellie made spaghetti and let me put as much cheese on top as I wanted. Stinky made me laugh so hard I almost spit noodles out my nose. He told a story about tripping over the garden hose and falling in the mud. Ellie said it was her favorite part of the day.

After dinner, I watched cartoons in a squishy pink bean bag chair. Ellie and Stinky sat on the couch, but they didn't make me talk if I didn't want to. They just let me be there.

When it was bedtime, Ellie tucked me in and asked if I needed anything.

"Do you want me to leave the door open a little?" she said.

"Yes, please."

She smiled. "Do you want Hopper to stand guard?"

"He always does," I whispered.

She gave me a kiss on the forehead. I didn't flinch. That surprised me.

When the lights went out, I hugged Hopper tight. The room didn't creak or smell like bleach. The sheets were warm. The house felt quiet but not scary.

And for the first time in a long time... I think I felt safe.

THREE

SURPRISES AND SECRETS

The next morning, the smell of bacon woke me up.

For a second, I forgot where I was. My eyes blinked open, and I saw the soft white ceiling and my pink bean bag chair in the corner. Then I remembered—I was at Ellie and Stinky's house now.

I jumped out of bed, grabbed Hopper, and tiptoed to the stairs. The closer I got, the louder my tummy rumbled.

"There's my sleepy girl!" Ellie said when she saw me. "You want to help set the table?"

I nodded and took a plate. It felt… nice. I liked helping.

We sat and ate together—eggs, bacon, toast, and grapes. I liked the grapes the most. Ellie said I could eat as many as I wanted. Nobody said I was eating too much. Nobody got mad if I made a mess. Stinky even dropped his fork and made a silly face like it had a mind of its own.

After breakfast, Ellie washed dishes and hummed a happy tune, while I colored at the table. Stinky went upstairs, and I heard thuds, like he dropped something.

I didn't mean to snoop. I just wanted to see what happened.

When I peeked into the room upstairs—the one with the rocking chair and baby blanket—Stinky was sitting on the floor. His face was red, and he wiped his eyes with his shirt. There was a broken picture frame near him and a little hole in the wall.

"Are you okay?" I whispered from the doorway.

He looked up, surprised. Then he sniffed and nodded. "Yeah, Mel. I just… missed something we never got to have."

I didn't really understand, but I knew what it was like to miss people and things. So I walked into the room and sat next to him. I held Hopper in my lap and gave him a quiet smile.

"You know," I said, "me and Hopper are good at listening."

He smiled back, and his eyes looked a little brighter.

Later, when Ellie came in, she knelt down and hugged him. She whispered something in his ear, and he nodded.

Then she looked at me and said, "How would you feel about painting this room any color you want someday?"

I blinked. "This one too?"

"Yep. We were thinking maybe… this could be your second room, or your playroom, or whatever you want."

"Can it be both?"

She laughed. "Of course it can."

And suddenly, that little warm feeling inside me got even bigger.

FOUR

ORANGE PAINT AND
PAPERWORK

The next few days were kinda like a dream.

We went to the paint store, and I got to pick any color I wanted for my room. Ellie told me I could even mix colors if I wanted. I told her I wanted it to look like a sunrise. "The real kind," I said. "With orange and gold and little bits of purple."

Stinky said, "We'll make your walls look like the sun woke up right next to your bed." That made me giggle so much I dropped the paint swatch.

They were weird in a good way. The kind of weird that felt like home.

Later that week, we all sat in this big room with other people. Some were quiet, some were whispering, and some looked like they were trying not to cry. I sat between Ellie and Levi, swinging my legs back and forth. I held Hopper tight.

A nice lady named Ms. Jones handed Ellie and Levi some papers. "We just need to get some information and do a few checks. Nothing scary," she said. "This is part of the adoption process."

Adoption. That word made my stomach do flip-flops. I had heard it before. Sometimes it meant "a forever family." But sometimes it meant, "another place I had to leave."

But when Ellie leaned over and whispered, "Don't worry, sweet pea. This is just the beginning," I kind of believed her.

They asked questions like, "Do you have locks on the cabinets?" and "Do you have enough beds?" and "Would you be willing to accept a child of any age?" I didn't know what most of that meant, but Levi answered kindly, and Ellie kept nodding with her serious face on.

After the meeting, we walked outside, and the wood floors creaked under our feet. I liked that sound. It was real. Not too quiet. Not too loud. Just like everything here.

When we got in the car, it was quiet for a while. Just the hum of the engine and the wind from the windows.

Then Ellie turned back to me and said, "Hey Mel? You know, if you ever want to talk about anything—anything at all—we're always here."

I didn't say anything right away. But I gave her a tiny smile and a nod.

Because I was starting to believe it was true.

FIVE

MISS LAURA IS BACK

The doorbell rang in the middle of the afternoon. Ellie went to open it while I stayed in my pink bean bag chair watching cartoons. I wasn't really paying attention... until I heard the voice.

"Hi, I'm here for the check-in," the lady said.

My head turned fast. I knew that voice. My stomach did a little flip.

I peeked around the corner—and there she was.

Miss Laura.

I hadn't seen her since before I came to Ellie and Stinky's house. She used to work at the place I stayed before, the one with the big white walls and too many rules. She helped with bedtime and always made me brush my teeth. She used to say I was her favorite, but she never called me Melanie.

She always called me Melody.

Ellie opened the door wider. "I thought Miss Jen would be doing the check-in."

"She's out sick," Miss Laura said quickly. "So I'm just filling in."

Ellie stepped aside and let her in, but I could tell something was off. Her smile didn't look real. It was too big. Too shiny. Too sharp.

She looked straight at me.

"There she is! Hi, Melody," she said.

I stood up slowly, clutching Hopper to my chest.

"It's Melanie," I corrected. I wasn't smiling.

She laughed like I was being silly. "Of course. Silly me."

Ellie asked her name again, and when she said "Laura," I saw Ellie's eyes flick toward Levi. He was standing in the hallway now too. Everyone was quiet for a second.

"Can I talk to her alone?" Miss Laura asked.

I didn't want to, but Ellie and Levi said it was okay. They didn't know. They didn't remember.

But I did.

Miss Laura sat on the couch beside me. Her perfume smelled the same as before—kind of like flowers and bleach. "I've missed you," she said, petting the edge of my sleeve. "I told everyone you were special. Didn't I always say that?"

I didn't answer. My mouth felt dry.

She smiled. "You know, I used to dream about taking you out for ice cream. Just us. Wouldn't that be nice?"

I didn't say anything. I wanted Ellie.

Miss Laura leaned closer. "Maybe we could do that sometime soon. Just you and me."

That's when I knew something was wrong.

Later, after she finally left, Ellie and Levi asked me questions. I told them Miss Laura used to take care of us at the home. I said she always called me Melody. I said she wanted to take me for ice cream by myself.

Ellie got very quiet. Levi's hands clenched into fists on the table.

I hugged Hopper that night so tight I thought his eye might pop off.

And even though I was safe in my room with the orange paint samples still sitting on my dresser...

I didn't feel safe anymore.

SIX

SOMETHING'S NOT RIGHT

After Miss Laura left, everything felt different. Not broken, just... tense. Like the house was holding its breath.

Ellie and Stinky didn't say much that night. They still made dinner—grilled cheese and tomato soup, my favorite—but they didn't joke around like usual. Ellie kept looking out the window. Levi's jaw was tight.

I didn't ask questions. I just dipped my sandwich and tried to act normal.

Later, while I watched TV, Ellie sat next to me and ran her fingers through my hair. "Hey, Mel," she said softly. "If someone ever asks you to go somewhere without me or Levi, what do you do?"

I blinked at the TV, pretending to still watch.

"I tell you first," I said.

"Exactly." She kissed the top of my head. "You're very smart."

I hugged Hopper tighter and nodded.

That night, I had a hard time falling asleep. I kept thinking I heard footsteps outside my window. Once, I swore I saw a shadow move across the wall, but it was probably just a car.

Probably.

The next day, I heard Ellie on the phone. She was outside on the porch, pacing back and forth. I peeked out through the blinds. Her face looked serious—more serious than when she talked to Ms. Jones or the doctor people.

When she came back in, she smiled like everything was fine. But her eyes weren't smiling.

"Want to go on a little trip?" she asked, way too cheerfully.

I paused. "Like... a vacation?"

She nodded. "Yep. Just the three of us. We'll bring Hopper too, of course."

I should've been excited. Trips meant hotel beds and restaurant ketchup bottles and getting to watch TV in the morning.

But instead, my chest felt tight.

Because I remembered what happened the last time Miss Laura showed up at a house I lived in.

And the way Ellie said "just the three of us" sounded more like a plan than a vacation.

Still, I nodded and packed my favorite PJs.

Because if Ellie and Stinky were going, I was going too.

SEVEN

THE VACATION THAT WASN'T

We left early in the morning.

Ellie helped me zip up my suitcase while Stinky packed the car. Hopper sat right on top, poking his little turtle head out like he was ready for an adventure.

"Where are we going?" I asked, sliding my arms into my hoodie.

Ellie smiled, but it looked a little too tight. "Akron. They've got an art museum and a zoo."

I nodded. That sounded fun. But I could feel something underneath her voice. It felt like when grown-ups pretend they're not mad, but you can still feel it in your stomach.

The drive was mostly quiet. Stinky turned the radio on, but nobody sang along this time. Ellie held his hand and kept looking at me in the back seat like she was checking to see if I was okay. I gave her a little thumbs-up and leaned against the window.

I watched the trees fly by. Some had flowers, some didn't. It looked like everything couldn't decide if it was spring or still winter.

After a while, I got sleepy. When I woke up, I was tilted sideways and my neck hurt. Ellie reached back and moved my head onto a pillow.

"We're almost there," she whispered.

At the hotel, everything smelled like cinnamon and floor cleaner. The bed was soft and bouncy, and the TV had a bunch of channels we didn't have at home. Stinky let me jump on the bed once before Ellie said, "Okay, that's enough wild monkey time."

At dinner, I ordered a cheeseburger and fries and extra ketchup. Ellie ordered a salad but only ate like three bites. Stinky made my ketchup packet into a heart shape and pretended it was a masterpiece.

I laughed, but I could tell he was trying too hard.

That night, something weird happened.

I woke up when I heard a noise. It was loud—like something fell in the hallway. I sat up quick, heart thumping like a drum. Stinky peeked through the hotel door, then came back and told us it was nothing, just someone with a cart.

But after he got in bed again, there was a knock.

Another one.

He went to the door again, and this time he came back holding a tiny folded piece of paper.

I asked what it said.

He looked at Ellie. "Not now."

They tucked me back in and whispered for a while in the bathroom. I pretended to be asleep, but I wasn't.

Later that night, I dreamed that Miss Laura was standing outside the hotel room door, smiling with her lips closed and her eyes too wide.

When I opened the door in the dream, she didn't say anything.

She just reached for my hand.

EIGHT

THE QUESTION I WASN'T
SUPPOSED TO ASK

The next morning, Stinky and I woke up before Ellie did.

I was already wide awake and hungry, so I poked him on the arm until he groaned and sat up. "Come on, Stinky," I whispered. "Let's go get breakfast."

We slipped out of bed while Ellie stayed curled up under the covers. She looked tired. I didn't want to wake her.

Stinky and I walked down the hotel hallway in our pajamas, laughing about how I had monster hair. He let me pick whatever I wanted from the breakfast bar: a muffin, a banana, and a little cup of cereal. He even carried a tray with coffee for Ellie and two orange juices for us.

I felt almost normal again. Almost.

We walked back to the room. I held Hopper in one arm and a bag of mini donuts in the other.

Stinky unlocked the door.

I walked in first. But forgot to hold the door. The door hit Stinky and he almost dropped the food.

"Oops, I'm sorry!" I quickly grabbed the door so he could walk in. We sit down to eat breakfast.

Nobody talked about the noise from last night. Or the note. Or how Ellie had her phone in her hand all morning like she was waiting for it to ring.

I stayed quiet for a long moment, my heart thumping in my chest like it was trying to get out. I didn't know everything, but I knew enough.

Ellie's phone rang.

She answered right away. "Mrs Jones?" Her voice was sharp and fast now. "Have you heard anything? Because she showed up again. Yes. At our house… then at the hotel." She got up and walked into the bathroom, closing the door halfway.

I looked at Stinky.

"She's going to help us," he said, but his voice was flat. "We're gonna leave the hotel. Go somewhere safer for a bit."

I blinked. "So… we're not staying here tonight?"

He shook his head. "No. We're going home. But the police will be watching the house this time. You'll be safe, I promise."

Ellie came out a minute later, already grabbing her bag. Her face looked pale, but her voice was strong. "Mel, sweet pea, I want you to grab your things, okay? Just your favorites. We're heading home."

I nodded and zipped Hopper into my backpack like we practiced during fire drills at school.

Everything felt fast after that—like the day got pushed into fast-forward. We packed. We checked out. Ellie signed something at the front desk while Stinky waited beside the car. I stayed in the back seat, hugging my knees.

I didn't ask any more questions.

NINE

NOT FAR ENOUGH

The ride home felt different than the ride to the hotel.

Nobody talked much. Ellie kept checking the rearview mirror like she was expecting someone to be behind us. Stinky had his arm on the back of my seat, but he wasn't saying his usual goofy stuff. He just kept clearing his throat and staring out the window.

I hugged Hopper tight in my lap, watching trees blur by.

When we pulled into our driveway, a police car was already parked out front. The officer standing beside it waved at us. He looked normal — not scary — but still, it made everything feel more real.

They really thought someone might come for us.

For me.

Ellie thanked the officer. He nodded and walked the perimeter of the house while we went inside. She turned on every light, even though it was still daytime. I heard her and Stinky checking all the windows and doors again.

I stayed in the middle of the living room, like I didn't know where to go.

"Mel," Ellie said gently, "do you want to help me make lunch?"

I shook my head. "Can I just sit here?"

"Of course, sweet pea."

She kissed the top of my head and went into the kitchen.

I looked around the house. It was still the same. My pink beanbag chair. The crayon drawing of me, Ellie, and Stinky hanging by the fridge. Hopper's extra turtle shell blanket on the couch.

But it didn't feel the same anymore.

After lunch, I went upstairs to my room. I looked out the window, just because I always do. The police car was still there.

But then I saw something strange.

Across the street, next to a tree, was a person.

They were too far away to see clearly. Just someone standing... still. Not walking. Not doing anything. Just watching the house.

My whole body froze.

I wanted to tell Ellie, but when I blinked and looked again, they were gone.

Maybe it was nothing.

Maybe it was a shadow or someone walking a dog.

But my heart didn't believe that.

Later, when Ellie tucked me in, I didn't tell her about the person. I wanted to. I almost did.

But I was afraid she'd look out the window and see nothing, and then maybe they wouldn't believe me.

So I hugged Hopper under the covers and whispered to him in the dark:

"She's not done."

TEN

ANOTHER NOTE

It was the next morning, and the house smelled like cinnamon oatmeal. Ellie always made it on Saturdays. She said it was a "slow morning food." But this morning didn't feel slow.

The police car was still outside. A different officer this time. He nodded at us through the window while sipping something from a big blue thermos.

I sat at the table eating my oatmeal quietly. Stinky scrolled on his phone. Ellie kept staring at the front door.

Then the doorbell rang.

I jumped. We all jumped.

Ellie answered it this time. I crept into the hallway, listening.

"Hello?" she asked.

"Hey, Mrs. Kelsh," the mailman said. "I have this letter for you. Just wanted to make sure you got it directly."

That was weird. Mail usually went in the box. Not to the door.

I peeked around the corner and saw him hand Ellie a plain white envelope. She stared at it like it had teeth.

"Thanks," she said, and shut the door.

She didn't open it right away. She stood there, holding it in both hands.

"Levi!" she called up the stairs. Her voice didn't sound scared, exactly. But it was close.

He came down fast. When he saw the envelope, he didn't even ask what it was.

He took it from her, opened it slowly, and read it.

I watched them from the hallway.

Ellie's hand went to her mouth.

Levi's jaw clenched.

"Mel," Ellie said, turning toward me. "Why don't you go upstairs for a minute, sweet pea?"

"What does it say?" I asked.

They didn't answer.

So I stayed put.

Ellie knelt down and took both my hands in hers.

"She says... she's still watching," she whispered. "And she used your old name again."

I knew what that meant.

Melody.

I felt the back of my neck go cold.

"She gave the note to the mailman?" I asked.

Ellie nodded slowly. "She must've. Which means... she's been close. Really close."

I didn't ask if the police saw her.

I already knew the answer.

I didn't cry.

But I wanted to scream.

Because now it wasn't just a scary story or a shadow in a dream.

She was real.

And she knew exactly where to find me.

ELEVEN

WAITING

Ellie was holding the envelope like it was made of glass. I watched her slide it into her purse, her mouth pressed into a flat line. Stinky stood by the door, car keys already in his hand. He looked like he was trying to be calm.

I wasn't sure it was working.

"Mel," Ellie said gently, crouching in front of me, "Levi and I need to go to the police station to talk about the note."

I nodded, but my stomach felt heavy. "Am I going with you?"

"No, sweet pea. Ms. Jones is coming to stay with you. Just for a little while."

I wanted to say no. I wanted to say don't leave me. But I didn't. I just nodded again and squeezed Hopper tight against my chest.

The doorbell rang. It was Ms. Jones, smiling with her soft pink lipstick and clipboard tucked under one arm. She knelt down and gave me a little wave.

"Hey there, superstar. Think you can keep me company for a bit?"

I gave a small smile. "I guess so."

Ellie kissed my forehead and whispered, "We'll be back soon. Call us if you need anything, okay?"

Stinky leaned down and bumped his forehead lightly against mine. "You've got Hopper as your bodyguard. And Ms. Jones. That's a dream team."

I didn't laugh. Not this time.

When they left, I sat on the couch next to Ms. Jones while she flipped through some papers.

"So," she said, "what should we do while we wait? Color? Watch a movie?"

"Can we just sit?" I asked.

"Of course."

We didn't say much for a while. The house was too quiet without Ellie and Stinky walking around, bumping into furniture and talking over each other. Even the clock ticking in the kitchen sounded louder.

I looked out the window. The police car was still out front, parked like a guard dog. I wondered if they knew about the note. I wondered if they believed it.

I wondered if Miss Laura was watching the house right now.

"Do you think she's coming back?" I asked, barely a whisper.

Ms. Jones paused. Then she turned to me, her face soft but serious. "I don't know. But I do know you're not alone. You're safe here. You've got a lot of grown-ups looking out for you now."

I nodded, even though I didn't feel safe.

I kept thinking about the name on the note.

Melody.

I hated how it looked. Like she was writing to someone who wasn't me.

I wasn't her.
I wasn't Melody.
I was Melanie.
And I wanted her to stop.

TWELVE

THE PLAN

It felt like forever before I heard the front door open.

I was sitting at the kitchen table with Ms. Jones, coloring in one of her grown-up work folders. She said I could draw on the back of the paper if I wanted — "better art than reports," she joked.

But I wasn't really drawing.

I was waiting.

When the door opened, I heard Ellie first. Her voice wasn't loud, but it was fast. I jumped up from my chair before Ms. Jones could even stand and ran toward the hallway.

Ellie dropped her purse and wrapped her arms around me.

"Hey, baby," she whispered into my hair. "I missed you."

Stinky followed behind her and gave Ms. Jones a small nod, the kind grown-ups do when they don't want to say anything in front of a kid.

But I wasn't just a kid.

"What happened?" I asked.

They looked at each other. I saw that look. It was the do-we-tell-her look.

Ellie crouched down to my level.

"They know it was Miss Laura who sent the note," she said. "And they believe us now. They're going to help keep you safe."

"How?" I asked.

"There will be police outside the house all day and night," she said. "They're tracking her now, using traffic cameras, buses — everything. They're watching."

"What if she's already here?" I whispered.

"They don't think she's close right now," Levi said. "But just in case... we're not going to let you out of our sight."

Ms. Jones stood up and gently closed her folder. "They're doing everything they can, Mel. And so are we."

I looked down at Hopper in my arms. He looked a little scruffy — like he'd been through a storm with me.

"We have to make a plan," I said quietly.

Ellie blinked. "What kind of plan, sweet pea?"

"Like... if she shows up. What do we do? Do I hide? Do I run? Do I scream?"

Her eyes got shiny again. She hated when I talked like that.

But I needed to.

Stinky sat beside me at the table. "Okay," he said. "Let's make a plan."

He pulled out a notepad and a pen.

"If anyone comes near the house who doesn't belong, you tell us immediately. If you ever feel unsafe, you come straight to one of us. You never go anywhere alone. Even to the mailbox."

"And Hopper comes everywhere," I added.

"Of course," Ellie smiled softly.

They wrote it all down.

Our safety plan.

It made me feel... not brave exactly, but ready. And that was close enough.

That night, when they tucked me into bed, I didn't ask them to leave the light on.

Just the door cracked, a little.

And Hopper sitting upright, like a guard.

Because for the first time since everything started, I didn't just feel like something bad was coming.

I felt like maybe we could face it.

Together.

THIRTEEN

CAUGHT

We were all in the living room when Ellie's phone rang.

She had been folding laundry that didn't really need folding, and Stinky was on the floor trying to fix the wheel on the wobbly coffee table. I was laying on the couch with Hopper on my chest, pretending to read but really just watching the ceiling fan spin.

The phone buzzed once. Twice. Ellie snatched it up so fast it made me sit up.

"Hello?" she answered. "Yes. This is her."

There was a long pause.

She didn't speak again for almost a minute.

Then she whispered, "Are you sure?"

She was nodding. Her eyes got wet, but she didn't blink.

Levi stood up. "What is it?" he mouthed.

Ellie finally spoke. "And where was she found?"

Another pause. A shorter one.

"Okay. Yes. Thank you. Please let us know."

She hung up and looked at us—at both of us—and even though she opened her mouth, the words didn't come right away.

"She's been caught," she finally said. "Laura."

My stomach jumped like it forgot how to sit still. "What do you mean caught?"

"She's in custody," Ellie said. "The police have her. She's not out there anymore."

I exhaled without meaning to. It came out sharp, shaky. My arms hugged Hopper tighter.

"She's gone?" I asked. "For real?"

"For real," Levi said, but his voice wasn't celebrating.

"Where?" I asked. "Where did they find her?"

Ellie and Levi looked at each other.

"They wouldn't say," Levi said. "Just that she's being held. Somewhere. Safe. Far from here."

I wanted to believe that. I really did.

But it was hard to believe in things when they didn't come with details.

FOURTEEN

THE PAPER THAT
MEANS FOREVER

After they caught Miss Laura, everything felt quieter.

Not right away. Not magically. But different. The kind of quiet that slowly started to feel safe again.

The police still drove by sometimes, and I still looked over my shoulder when we walked down the sidewalk. But the air around our house didn't feel like it was holding its breath anymore.

It felt like it could finally exhale.

One morning, about two weeks later, Ellie called me into the kitchen.

She was sitting at the table with a stack of papers. Levi stood behind her with two mugs of tea and a giant cinnamon roll he said we had to "eat with serious ceremony."

I climbed into my usual chair, hugging Hopper in my lap.

"What is all that?" I asked, pointing at the papers.

Ellie smiled. Not her worried smile. A real one.

"This," she said, sliding the top sheet toward me, "is the adoption paperwork. It's been approved. All of it."

My heart skipped.

"You mean... it's really happening?"

"It's really happening," Levi said. "Court date's in two weeks. Then you're officially stuck with us forever."

I laughed. I couldn't help it. It bubbled out of me before I even understood why.

Ellie reached across the table and took my hand. "You don't have to be scared anymore, Melanie. No one's coming to take you away. No one can."

I looked down at the paper. It had my name on it.

But not the name she used.

Not Melody.

It said Melanie June Kelsh.

My name. My real name.

I ran my fingers over the letters like they might fade if I didn't hold onto them fast enough.

That night, I helped Ellie bake cookies. We burned the first batch, but Levi ate them anyway and said they tasted like "justice." I laughed until my face hurt.

And later, when Ellie tucked me in, I didn't ask her to leave the door open.

I didn't need her to.

Because now, even with the lights off, I knew where I was.

I was home.

FIFTEEN

ADOPTION DAY

The courthouse didn't look anything like I thought it would.

There were no marble columns or golden doors. Just a big glass building with metal detectors at the front and grown-ups in suits who talked too fast.

But somehow, it still felt important.

Like something was about to happen that would change everything.

We walked down a long hallway together — me, Ellie, and Levi. Ellie was wearing a soft blue dress that made her look like spring. Levi wore his "serious grown-up shirt" but still had mustard on his sleeve. I wore the outfit Ellie let me pick out: yellow skirt, white sneakers, and a sparkly clip in my hair that made me feel brave.

I held Hopper tight. He was freshly washed, his little shell still damp.

When we got to the courtroom, there were people waiting. Ms. Jones. Miss Jen. Even the officer who used to sit outside our house. They all smiled when they saw me.

The judge sat up at the front in a black robe. He looked like someone who didn't smile much — but when I walked in with Ellie and Levi, his whole face softened.

"Is this our future Kelsh?" he asked.

Everyone laughed. Even me.

We sat down, and the judge asked some questions — to Ellie and Levi, mostly.

"Do you promise to raise her as your daughter?"

"Yes."

"Do you understand this means forever?"

"Yes."

Then he looked at me.

"Melanie," he said. "Do you want to be adopted by these two?"

I nodded hard. "Yes, please."

"Why?" he asked gently.

I blinked. No one told me I'd have to answer.

But the words came anyway.

"Because they kept me safe," I said. "And because I'm not scared when I'm with them. And because they call me by my real name."

The judge smiled.

"I think that's a pretty good reason," he said, and signed the paper.

Just like that, it was done.

Everyone clapped. Ellie cried. Levi picked me up in a bear hug so big Hopper almost fell out of my arms.

And I — I just smiled so big it felt like it came out of my chest.

When we walked out of the building, someone handed me a balloon that said Forever Family in pink letters. Ellie let me hold the papers myself, the ones with my new name printed clear across the top:

Melanie June Kelsh.

We went out for ice cream after. Not the kind where I had to pretend I was someone else. Not the kind where I had to look over my shoulder.

The real kind.

The kind you eat when you know you're never going anywhere again.

FINAL NOTE

HOPPER KNOWS

Sometimes, I still wake up thinking I'm somewhere else.

Like the old places—cold sheets, whispers through thin walls, the smell of bleach and plastic bowls. But then I open my eyes, and there's my room. The orange paint I picked. The bookshelf Levi built. The turtle lamp on my dresser.

And Hopper. Still here.

He's a little more worn now. One eye is loose. His stuffing's kind of lumpy in the middle.

But he knows everything.

He knows what it felt like to be called the wrong name, and what it meant to finally hear the right one.

He knows how scary it was when no one believed me—and how good it felt when Ellie did.

He knows how many nights I pretended I was brave before I actually was.

He was there when I ran, when I hid, when I fought to stay.

He was there the day the paper said forever.

And he's here now, sitting on my pillow while I write this. I'm older, but not so old I don't need him anymore.

Not so old that I've forgotten.

Sometimes, people ask me how I made it through.

And I don't always know how to answer.

But if I could go back and tell the girl I used to be—curled up in the corner of another strange room, holding Hopper like a shield—I'd say this:

"It gets better.

You'll get safe.

You'll get loud.

You'll get to keep your name.

You'll get to stay.

And one day, when you wake up,

You won't be afraid anymore."

And when that day comes?

You'll know it.

Because Hopper will be smiling.

Just like you.

www.ingramcontent.com/pod-product-compliance
Lightning Source LLC
Chambersburg PA
CBHW031856170626
46807CB00004B/1763